For Guy Brendan —M. R.
For Theo —L. L.

Published by
PEACHTREE PUBLISHERS
1700 Chattahoochee Avenue
Atlanta, Georgia 30318-2112
www.peachtree-online.com

Text © 2013 by Michelle Robinson
Illustrations © 2013 by Leonie Lord

First published in Great Britain in 2013 by Orchard Books
First United States version published in 2013 by Peachtree Publishers

The illustrations were rendered digitally.

Printed in April 2013 in China
10 9 8 7 6 5 4 3 2 1
First Edition

Library of Congress Cataloging-in-Publication Data
Robinson, Michelle (Michelle Jane), 1977-
Ding dong! gorilla! / text by Michelle Robinson ; illustrations by Leonie Lord.
    pages cm
Summary: "A little boy has a lot of explaining to do when a gorilla comes over and makes a mess of
the house...but that's not even the bad news"—Provided by publisher.
    ISBN-13: 978-1-56145-730-4
    ISBN-10: 1-56145-730-2
[1. Gorilla—Fiction. 2. Behavior—Fiction. 3. Humorous stories.] I. Lord, Leonie, illustrator. II. Title.
PZ7.R567535Di 2013
[E]—dc23
                                    2012048851

DING DONG! GORILLA!

MICHELLE ROBINSON LEONIE LORD

PEACHTREE
ATLANTA

You know we ordered a pizza?

A GREAT **BIG**

ONE WITH **EXTRA** CHEESE?

Well, I'm afraid I have some BAD news . . .

YOU SEE, while you were upstairs getting ready for dinner, the doorbell rang.

DING

DONG!

I thought
it must be
the pizza boy,
so I answered it.

It was
DEFINITELY
NOT
the
PIZZA
BOY.

I didn't invite the gorilla in.
He just barged right past me.

He went straight to my
TOY BOX
and dumped everything
out to get at the
CRAYONS.

He did LOTS of **COLORING**, but he wasn't very good at staying between the lines.

But that's not the **BAD** NEWS.

When the gorilla got bored, he **STOMPED OFF** to watch TV.

He went through all my movies,
but at least he put them
away afterward.

JUST NOT IN THE RIGHT PLACES...

That's not the BAD news, either.

Next, the gorilla wanted to play dress up.

I COULDN'T STOP HIM!

He put on all my clothes (and most of yours, too).

THEN
HE LEFT
THEM IN A
DIRTY
PILE
ON MY BEDROOM FLOOR.

But even that's not such bad news.

At least he washed

SOME of

them.

I thought perhaps the gorilla was overexcited,
so I sent him outside to get some fresh air . . .

. . . but he got some fresh flowers instead.
The garden doesn't look so pretty anymore.

The gorilla wanted to play

SOCCER

next, but it was getting dark.

So we came
back inside.

It wasn't me
who broke the

VASE...

or the
WINDOW...

or the chair.

And that STILL
isn't the BAD news.

By now the gorilla was GETTING REALLY **HUNGRY**. I was a bit scared, but he wasn't interested in me.

He wanted to bake a **CHOCOLATE CAKE**.

THIS TIME IT **REALLY** **WAS** the **PIZZA** **BOY.**

He looked
surprised to see us.

He ran away before
I could pay him.

I suppose that's quite

GOOD

news, really.

The gorilla ran
away when he heard
you coming downstairs.

So you probably won't
believe that HE made
all this mess.

You are BOUND to
blame me and send
me to bed without
any pizza.

But the
BAD
news is…

PIZZA